DPT

ALLEN COUNTY PUBLIC LIBRARY
FORT WAYNE, INDIANA 46802

You may return this book to any location of
the Allen County Public Library.

DEMCO

Put Beginning Readers on the Right Track with
ALL ABOARD READING™

The All Aboard Reading series is especially for beginning readers. Written by noted authors and illustrated in full color, these are books that children really and truly *want* to read—books to excite their imagination, tickle their funny bone, expand their interests, and support their feelings. With four different reading levels, All Aboard Reading lets you choose which books are most appropriate for your children and their growing abilities.

Picture Readers—for Ages 3 to 6
Picture Readers have super-simple texts with many nouns appearing as rebus pictures. At the end of each book are 24 flash cards—on one side is the rebus picture; on the other side is the written-out word.

Level 1—for Preschool through First Grade Children
Level 1 books have very few lines per page, very large type, easy words, lots of repetition, and pictures with visual "cues" to help children figure out the words on the page.

Level 2—for First Grade to Third Grade Children
Level 2 books are printed in slightly smaller type than Level 1 books. The stories are more complex, but there is still lots of repetition in the text and many pictures. The sentences are quite simple and are broken up into short lines to make reading easier.

Level 3—for Second Grade through Third Grade Children
Level 3 books have considerably longer texts, use harder words and more complicated sentences.

All Aboard for happy reading!

For my editor, Judy Donnelly—L.H.

To my Dad, who gave me the art spirit—G.G.D.

Special thanks to Benjamin Wolpoff for his help with this book.

Text copyright © 1997 by Linda Hayward. Illustrations copyright © 1997 by Gabriela Dellosso. All rights reserved. Published by Grosset & Dunlap, Inc., a member of The Putnam & Grosset Group, New York. ALL ABOARD READING is a trademark of The Putnam & Grosset Group. GROSSET & DUNLAP is a trademark of Grosset & Dunlap, Inc. Published simultaneously in Canada. Printed in the U.S.A.

Library of Congress Cataloging-in-Publication Data
Hayward, Linda.
    Cave people / Linda Hayward : illustrated by Gabriela Dellosso.
        p. cm.—(All aboard reading. Level 2)
    Summary: Discusses who the Neanderthals were, when and how they lived, and how we know about them.
    1. Neanderthals—Juvenile literature. [1. Neanderthals. 2. Prehistoric peoples.] I. Dellosso, Gabriela, ill. II. Title III. Series.
    GN285. H39 1997
    569.9—dc21   97-15295
                                                                                                          CIP
ISBN 0-448-41337-X (GB) A B C D E F G H I J   AC
ISBN 0-448-41336-1 (pbk) A B C D E F G H I J

ALL
ABOARD
READING™

Level 2
Grades 1-3

CAVE PEOPLE

By Linda Hayward
Illustrated by Gabriela Dellosso

Grosset & Dunlap • New York

It is fifty thousand years ago.

These hunters are hungry.

They need meat.

They see a mammoth.

But it is too big for them to hunt.

The men hide until it goes away.

These hunters have spotted a reindeer!
The hunters come closer.

The reindeer tries to fight back.

But the hunters kill it with their spears.

Who are these hunters?

They are called Neanderthals.

(You say it like this: nee-AN-der-thals.)

These people lived in caves

long, long ago.

It was the Ice Age—

the time of the mammoth

and the cave bear.

Winters were long and dark.

Even the summers were cold.

The Neanderthals had big teeth
and low foreheads.
They had bony ridges
above their eyes.
Their bodies
were short and thick.
The Neanderthals
really did not look
that different from people today.
But they were probably
much stronger.
They had to be.

Life was hard.
Neanderthals spent much
of their time finding food
and just trying to stay alive.

A lion could spring out of nowhere!
Neanderthals had to be ready
for all kinds of dangers.

Neanderthals lived
in small groups.
Women, men, children—
about twenty people in all.
Everyone took care of each other.
This made the group strong.

This man has broken a rib.

Someone will feed him

and protect him until he is well.

Neanderthals felt safe inside a cave.
Of course they checked the cave
for cave bears before they moved in!

The women kept a fire burning

all day and all night.

It was nice and warm.

The fire lit up the dark cave walls.

The fire scared away wolves and lions.

Inside the cave there was a place

for sleeping.

Soft, furry animal skins made good beds.

More skins were hung over

the cave opening.

The skins kept out the wind

and snow and rain.

Skins could also be turned into clothing.
Neanderthals wore mammoth skins
and bear hides and fox pelts.

They made holes in the skins
and laced them together.
They even made leather wrappings
for their feet.
They needed warm clothes
when they went outside to hunt.

Hunting was dangerous.

Bears had claws.

Mammoths had tusks.

Bisons had horns.

Hunters had to get up close

to use their spears.

If they weren't careful,

they could get killed!

These hunters are lucky.

They have found an animal

killed by a lion.

But the hunters must be quick.

The lion might come back!

There's just enough time

to slice off some meat

and take it to a safer place.

Some Neanderthals

put fresh meat in ice pits.

The frozen meat lasted a long time.

These were the first refrigerators!

Frozen meat was rock hard.

Raw meat was tough.

Some Neanderthals roasted meat

over a fire.

Sometimes they made cooking pits.

They put the meat inside the pits

with hot stones from the fire.

They covered it all with dirt.

Hours later, the meat was warm and tender.

What else was on
the Ice Age menu?

Toasted beetles.

Roasted turtle.

Fresh cattails.

Chopped roots.

Burnt reindeer meat.

Bison brain stew.

Neanderthals were smart.

They knew how to make tools

for different jobs.

Tools for cutting meat and carving wood
and making holes and scraping skins.

This man is making a slicer.

He wants to use it to cut meat.

First he finds a good piece of flintstone.

Then he strikes it with a rock.

He has to hit just the right spot.

A flake breaks off.

The man hammers the flake

to make it jagged and sharp.

He hits it over a hundred times!

How do we know about Neanderthals?

Scientists dig up their bones.

They find their tools.

They study the caves where they lived.

Some scientists even try

to make stone tools

the way the cave people did.

They learn what a hard job it was!

Sometimes scientists find

Neanderthal graves.

These bones show that the body

was placed carefully in its grave.

There are bits of flowers on the bones.

This means that someone

put flowers on the dead body.

Today we too put flowers

on people's graves.

Neanderthals did not live very long.

Forty-five years was a long life.

People got sick.

Some starved.

Some froze.

There were also floods
and earthquakes.

These Neanderthals

were in their cave

when an earthquake struck.

The ground trembled.

Rocks and dirt tumbled down

from the cave ceiling.

Most of the people got out.

But some were buried inside.

Fifty thousand years later,
scientists will dig up the buried bones.
The bones are clues
about how Neanderthals lived.

Still, there is much

we do not know about Neanderthals.

What did they think about?

What did they believe?

Neanderthals left

no pictures on cave walls,

no writing on stones.

We can only guess about

what they felt and thought.

Neanderthals probably had words

for things—

things that they could point to.

Places, people, animals, plants.

But could they count to twenty?

Name the colors in a rainbow?

Tell about their dreams?

Maybe.

We don't know for sure.

The biggest mystery is:

What happened to the Neanderthals?

They were around for two hundred

thousand years.

During that time they were

the smartest creatures on earth.

Then about thirty-five thousand years ago,

they began to disappear.

A few thousand years later

all the Neanderthals were gone.

The world was filling up

with a new kind of people—

the people you see here.

Why did the Neanderthals disappear?
Scientists want to find out.
Maybe the answer will tell us
something about ourselves.